Here Comes the Showboat!

Here Comes

Written and Illustrated by

ELLIS CREDLE

the Showboat!

THOMAS NELSON & SONS

Edinburgh NEW YORK Toronto

Books Written and Illustrated by Ellis Credle

DOWN DOWN THE MOUNTAIN
ACROSS THE COTTON PATCH
LITTLE JEEMES HENRY
PEPÉ AND THE PARROT

Acknowledgment is made to *Story Parade*, where this first appeared in a shorter version, in the issues of March, April, May and June, 1948, under the title
WAY DOWN YONDER IN PASQUOTANK

Printed in the United States of America by H. WOLFF, New York

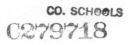
To
a little boy who wanted
a pair of cowboy boots—
my brother

CONTENTS

ILLUSTRATIONS

Here Comes the Showboat!

1. The Jumping Frogs

CHRISTOPHER and Lucy Gale lived in a great old house that looked out over the Pasquotank River. It had been washed to a gray silvery color by many years of wind and rain, and its shingles were velvety green with moss.

From its long upper porch they could look out over the low flat countryside. Ditches and canals that crisscrossed the fields this way and that, made a great checkerboard down below, a checkerboard whose squares turned different colors with each change of the seasons. In the fall there were squares of white cotton and squares of yellow corn; in the spring, squares of black plowed land and squares of bright green sprouting crops. After a long rain the checkerboard disappeared beneath a shining sheet of water that stood everywhere, making it easy for Chris and Lucy to pretend their upper porch was the deck of a sailing vessel surrounded by the wide ocean. But the water did not stay long. It was soon carried away to the Pasquotank River by all the ditches and canals.

An avenue of gnarled old live oaks, like bearded bent old men in rusty green coats, led from the house down to the road that wound lazily away to the little village of Bayview.

On the far edge of the wide green lawn was the family graveyard, where other Gales were buried. It was a quiet solemn place, enclosed by dark clumps of boxwood that gave off a pungent smell like incense. The old stones leaned toward each other as if whispering together of times long past. Lucy, who liked to hear the tales the old folks told of great times in these North Carolina lowlands, often went there to read the words on the tombstones and to dream of days long ago.

The first of those long-ago Gales had come to build ships from the towering cypress trees, the tall pines and splendid hard cedars that grew there. For more than a hundred years, the forests had rung with the sound of axes, hammers and saws, as the trees fell and the ships were built. North Carolina became famous for those slim, fast little sailing vessels. They skimmed the ocean like white-winged birds, carrying Carolina tar pitch and turpentine to the far-away Caribbean Islands, returning with shiploads of sugar, rum and molasses.

The Gales of those days had been busy and rich. The house that Chris and Lucy lived in had been built then. Their furniture had been bought then, too—carved mahogany settees, slender tables, graceful chairs that had been brought from England.

The old stones leaned toward each other.

But now all was quiet on the Pasquotank. The days of
sailing ships were over. The great modern vessels of steel
and iron could not pass the long sandbanks that lay like
fortifications all along the Carolina coasts. The splendid
timbers of the lowlands were all cut away.

There was not much money left in the Gale family.
They had the old house and the land. With the help of a
Negro family—Uncle Benny, Aunt Selina and their four
sons—Papa raised a crop of cotton, corn and soybeans. It
gave everybody a living, but there was never any money to
spend.

But Chris and Lucy did not feel poor. Aunt Selina, who
helped Mama in the kitchen, made wonderful dumplings
from blackberries picked in the swamps around about,

15

cooked delicious fried chicken, and concocted tasty stews of crabs or fish caught in the river in front of their house. They had never been away from their swampland home, never seen a city, never heard the rattle of a train. But life did not seem dull to them. It was lively and full of fun.

Chris had a yearling calf named Zero, and a calf cart that he and Uncle Benny had made from two cast-off wagon wheels. Lucy had a doll named Mrs. La Tour, for whom she made elegant dresses from silk or gingham scraps. She had, besides, a lovely yellow mother cat, which had a new family of fancy-colored kittens every few months.

But *Skeeter*, their little rowboat, gave them more pleasure than anything else. What fun it was to climb into it on a bright sunny morning and row along the lead canal that passed through their father's fields! The canal was an exciting, mysterious stream. It flowed from the dark cypress swamp and its waters were stained as brown as coffee. Milk-white pond lilies floated on the dark water, their golden hearts open to the sun. Chris and Lucy guided their little boat carefully among the flowers, smelling the heavenly sweet perfume.

Great green bullfrogs stared at them from their holes along the bank and as they came near leaped into the water with a loud *ker-lump!* Jeweled dragonflies hovered about, perching lightly on the tip of a spiked rush, then darting swiftly away. They were the devil's-darning-needles, Aunt Selina told them.

Sometimes as they rowed silently along, dipping their oars quietly, they came upon a scoggin, a queer awkward bird, busily fishing for minnows. What handsome colors he wore! Slate-blue coat and henna vest. If he caught sight of them, he took to the air immediately with slow creaking wingbeat.

The little boat slid through the water.

But not all their trips on the canal were for pleasure alone. One summer afternoon Chris and Lucy set out in their little boat on an important mission. They sat side by side, each pulling manfully on a small oar. *Dip, dip, dip* went the oars, keeping perfect time, making the little boat slide smoothly through the water. They followed the canal to the place where it flowed into a creek, and turned into its broader, deeper waters.

The creek was as crooked as a blacksnake's path. First Chris, then Lucy, had to push back against the water with an oar, while the other rowed hard to make the boat go around the curve. A damp muddy smell rose from the marshes that stretched away gray and drab on either side, as far as the eye could see. The children looked constantly over their shoulders to see if they were headed properly toward Bayview. Lucy's straight blonde locks blew back with the salt wind, and Chris's waving yellow hair glistened in the sunlight. Their eyes shone with an eager light as they slid along.

At last the little cluster of housetops came into view. They could see the red roof of the schoolhouse, the white steeple of the church, and the fancy front of Mr. Midgett's General Store standing up above the rushes.

"We'll soon be there," said Lucy.

"Wonder how much I'll get for my frogs?" Chris said, glancing down into the bottom of the boat where a dozen frogs lay with feet tied together.

"I hope I'll get as much as twenty-five cents a dozen for my eggs," Lucy added.

Her gray eyes looked eager.

They rowed steadily. An otter, surprised by the splashing of their oars, dived from the bank and swam playfully about the boat, lifting a sleek furry head from the water to look at them with soft round eyes.

"Isn't he a show-off!" exclaimed Lucy. "Look at him shake his whiskers at us! Every time we come this way he has to jump in and show off his tricks."

The otter made a barrel roll in the water, glancing proudly at the children as if to say, "Just see what I can do!" Then he darted away to his muddy home among the rushes.

Once a snow-white egret flew up from the brown water and sailed away over the marshes.

"That's good luck," Lucy said. "A white bird means good

They edged carefully around the schooner.

luck. We'll get a good price for our things today, you wait and see!"

Chris and Lucy approached the village the back way by the creek. They rowed around the curves, past an old ruined sawmill, a busy buzzing cotton gin, the back yards of a few houses, and came at last to the wharf that led up to Midgett's General Store.

They edged carefully around the barnacled sides of an oyster schooner that was anchored there, then headed in to tie up to the wharf. Chris stood up and grasped the edge of the wharf to keep the boat from bumping. Lucy got the painter and tied it to a piling. Then they began to gather up the things they had come to sell. Chris lifted his bunch of bullfrogs; Lucy brought out her basket of eggs that she had stowed carefully underneath the stern seat.

"Hi, there!" said a voice, as they climbed out of the boat.

They looked up to see a head sticking out of the oyster boat's cabin.

"Hi, Mr. Silverthorne."

HERE COMES THE SHOWBOAT!

Mr. Silverthorne had mustaches like a walrus and a face like an old shriveled apple.

"What you young'uns up to today?" he inquired.

"Came to sell some frogs and some eggs, Mr. Silverthorne."

"Gee whillikers! You young'uns are always selling something. Must be making a pile of money! What you doing with all your money?"

"Oh, we're not telling," said Chris.

"Business secret, hey?"

"Yep," Chris replied.

"Bet you're going to buy that pair of cowboy boots you're always talking about."

"Well, I sure would like to have those boots," admitted Chris slowly. "But—but they're five dollars in the Sears, Roebuck catalog. It would take a month of Sundays to save that much money. Nope, this is for something else."

"Bet Lucy's going to get some furniture for that pretty dolly of hers."

Lucy looked wistful. There was nothing she wanted more than a little bed for Mrs. La Tour to sleep in, and a little bureau with a mirror in which she might look at herself. There was a whole bedroom set in the catalog, just the right thing for her dear Mrs. La Tour. But like Chris, she felt it would take years to earn the five dollars necessary to buy it. She shook her head and smiled at Mr. Silverthorne.

"No, it's not for doll furniture," she said.

"Well then, lemme sell you a bushel of oysters—finest oysters in Pasquotank!"

Mr. Silverthorne scooped up a great shovelful of wet oysters and held it poised, looking at them expectantly.

"Not today!" laughed the children.

They set off, trotting along the wharf toward the store.

Mr. Silverthorne popped back into his cabin on the boat.

Suddenly Chris paused, staring toward the shore.

"Say, who is that?" he exclaimed, frowning.

A strange man in citified clothes, and a young boy in a bright necktie, stood looking up at the side of an old warehouse near Midgett's Store.

"I hope it's not one of those traveling salesman," Chris said.

"Why don't you want to see a traveling salesman?" asked Lucy, peering at the strangers.

"Because they always make jokes about Pasquotank," Chris replied. "They holler that old rhyme, *Way down yonder in Pasquotank,* and all the rest of it. I'm sick and tired of it. I'm so sick and tired of it I feel just like busting somebody in the nose!"

"Shucks, they don't mean any harm," said Lucy. "They think it's a funny joke."

"After you've heard a joke a million times it's not funny any more," Chris said.

They walked slowly toward the store, casting curious looks at the two beside the warehouse. A new person seldom came to the Pasquotank country. It was far from the highway and no railroads came anywhere near it. All the people who lived there had been born there, and Chris and Lucy knew everyone almost as well as they knew their own mother and father. Outsiders looked strange to them.

These two people looked stranger than usual. The man had on a bright-colored suit with large checks. The boy wore bright tan shoes and a red-and-green tie. They seem to be engaged in some kind of queer business, too. The boy was stirring something in a big bucket. The man was unrolling some long strips of paper. On the ground beside them were brushes, the handles as long as the side of a house.

Still watching, but trying not to stare, Chris and Lucy crossed the dusty road. As they climbed the steps to the store, the man looked up. Catching sight of Chris's bunch of frogs, he sang out teasingly:

"Way down yonder in Pasquotank,
Where the bullfrogs jump from bank to bank!"

Mr. Midgett fell on his face.

Chris looked angry. He felt like fighting somebody. The boy, who was about Chris's size, looked up from the bucket and laughed aloud. The laugh was too much for Chris. Dropping his frogs, he sprang at the boy. He grabbed him by the necktie and drew back a fist threateningly.

"What are you laughing at?" he shouted.

The boy's eyes popped wide open. "N-n-n-nothing!" he stammered. "N-n-n-nothing!"

"What's the matter with Pasquotank? Can't the frogs jump from bank to bank if they want to? What's wrong with that? What's funny about it?"

"There's one!" screamed Lucy.

"N-n-n-nothing. N-n-n-nothing."

"Chris!" Lucy cried. "Look! Your frogs have got loose. They're all jumping away!"

Chris let go of the boy and made a dive for his frogs. They were jumping in all directions.

"Hey! Catch 'em!" he shouted. "They're headed for the water!"

"There's one!" yelled the boy with the red tie, and made a grab at the air.

The frog leaped again. The boy threw himself to the road and caught it by one leg.

"Hey, here's one!"

The man in the checked suit grabbed for another. He missed, grabbed again, and dashed after it, shouting.

"Help! There's one!" screamed Lucy. "He's headed for the water!"

She ran after it, and flung herself on it like a baseball player sliding for first base.

"Hey! What's the matter?" cried Mr. Midgett, running out onto his porch. "What's going on here?"

What he saw was a great cloud of dust, and people jumping around like lunatics, throwing themselves down on the ground, grabbing at the air and yelling. When at last he understood that everyone was grabbing for frogs, he ran down the steps and tried to help.

Mr. Midgett was a fat little man with a large round stomach. He reached for a jumping frog, lost his balance and fell on his face. The dust rolled in clouds as everybody rushed about shouting, tripping over each other, falling headlong as they reached for the leaping frogs.

At last there were no more frogs to be seen. Everybody stood up and looked at each other. They were greatly astonished. Nobody looked the same as when the scramble began.

"I got four!" exclaimed the stranger, holding up four goggle-eyed green frogs.

"I didn't get but two," said the boy.

"One, two, three, four," counted Chris. "I got four," he shouted triumphantly.

"Here's one," said Lucy, holding it out to Chris.

"I-gollies, I didn't get nary one," said the fat little store-keeper sorrowfully.

"All here but one," Chris said. "I had a dozen."

They looked at each other. Their clothes were dusty, their faces so black and dirty that their eyes looked white out of the dark skin.

"I-gollies, you sure do look funny!" Mr. Midgett snickered at Chris.

"Go in and take a look at the mirror," said Chris. "You look pretty funny yourself."

Then everybody laughed.

"Well, I reckon that's eleven frogs that won't do any more jumping from bank to bank," said the stranger.

"I—I sure do thank you for helping me to catch them," said Chris hesitantly. Then, turning to the boy who was holding his share of the catch, he said a little ashamedly, "I'm sorry I was so rough on you just now."

"Oh, that's all right," said the boy. "Forget it. I reckon I ought not to have teased you."

The strange man dusted his clothes and straightened his necktie.

"Well, get along with that paste, Delbert. We got to get this thing up and get going."

The boy went back to his bucket, and with a last curious glance at him Chris and Lucy followed Mr. Midgett into the store. The storekeeper took Lucy's basket of eggs and counted them, shaking each one to see if it was sound, then slipping it carefully into a little compartment in a large egg crate.

"One dozen eggs exactly," he said at last. "Twenty-five cents."

Then, one by one, he began to count Chris's frogs.

"Folks tell me that frogs' legs fried nice and brown taste just like chicken," he said. "But seems like I never had no hankering to taste 'em. They's too many of 'em hopping around the ditches. City folks likes 'em though, I reckon, or they wouldn't buy 'em. I'm shipping 'em down the river all the time."

He put the last frog into the crate and fastened the lid securely.

"Don't want these fellows jumping all over my store," he added. "If you was to get after 'em the way you did out there in the road, everything in the place would be busted clean to matchwood."

He looked down at Chris. "Well, you got eleven frogs," he said, "but tell you what, I'll make it twelve. Reckon it was my fault that last one got away. Thirty cents a dozen they are this week."

Chris and Lucy looked at each other and smiled. Twenty-five cents for her, thirty for him. They were having luck after all.

"Do you want the cash money," inquired Mr. Midgett, "or will you take something from the store?"

"We'll take the money, please, Mr. Midgett," Chris replied.

"Don't you want some candy?" asked the storekeeper temptingly. "I've got a new kind. It's got a sparkler in the handle. You wait until nighttime, set a match to it, and it just throws out all kinds of sparks. Real pretty! Looks like a whole flock of fireflies sparklin' over the marshes."

He held one out for them to see. Lucy examined it with shining eyes.

"Should we get just one?" she asked Chris breathlessly.

"Nope, ne'r a one," said Chris stoutly.

Lucy drew back and nodded agreement. They had something better in mind than mere fancy sparklers. Mr. Midgett looked disappointed.

"Never saw such young'uns in my life," he grumbled. "Can't sell 'em a thing. Always selling something but don't never buy nothing. If all my customers were like you, I'd end up in the poorhouse. What you doing with all your money?"

"We're saving it, Mr. Midgett," said Lucy.

"Saving it! I-gollies, you sure are! What you saving it for?"

"Oh, we're not telling," laughed Chris.

"Uncle Benny says it's bad luck to talk about your

plans," explained Lucy seriously. "Talk about 'em and talk is all they'll amount to. That's what he says."

"Plans? Plans? Now what kind of plans have you got up your sleeve?" Mr. Midgett scratched his head in a puzzled way. "I declare, you children have certainly got my curiosity up."

The children laughed as they pocketed their money and left the store. Outside a surprise awaited them. The boy with the bucket of paste and the man with the long-handled brush were nowhere to be seen, but covering one whole side of the warehouse where they had stood, was a bright and glowing picture.

COMING NEXT WEEK!

it announced in great tall letters. Underneath was a picture of a long flattop boat. And what a gorgeous boat it was! Painted white, trimmed in scarlet and gold, and fluttering with gay colored flags.

"The Showboat!" exclaimed Chris, and shouted for joy.

"It's coming!" cried Lucy.

Once a year, in the fall, this wonderful floating theater came moving slowly, proudly up the Pasquotank River, towed by a busy, puffing little tugboat. It tied up at the dock in front of Mr. Midgett's store, and people of the lonely marsh country were treated to the only shows they ever had a chance to see. For a whole week it stayed in Bayview and every night a different play was acted on its brightly lighted stage. Beautiful girls danced in gaily spangled dresses, a funny blackfaced comedian played the banjo and sang funny songs, and a magician did amazing, puzzling tricks. It was pure delight!

Chris and Lucy looked forward to it as they did to Christmas. As they stood gazing, they clasped their money happily. There was enough to buy tickets for every show. It was what they had been saving for.

"Look!" said Lucy, pointing. "There's something new this year. They're having a contest." She read:

OLD HOME SONG CONTEST!
FOR YOUNG AND OLD!
ANYBODY FROM SIX TO SIXTY!

Old Songs, New Songs, Funny Songs, Sad Songs!
Come up on the stage of the Showboat and try your
luck!

Win the Grand Prize!

$5.00 in gold awarded for the best song!

Come One! Come All!

"Five dollars in gold!" gasped Chris.

"Gee!" Lucy's eyes grew as round as silver dollars.

"Wouldn't you like to get that prize?" asked her brother.

"Let's try for it," said Lucy.

"Oh, we'd never get it," Chris said.

"We might," she replied stoutly. "You never can tell. We've been lucky today. We might be lucky then."

"Gee! Five dollars!" sighed Chris.

For a long time they stood gazing at the poster. Then, noticing that the sun was beginning to sink low across the marshes, they turned and walked slowly along the wharf toward their boat.

"Hi!" Mr. Silverthorne's head popped out of the cabin of his oyster boat.

"Oh!" Chris and Lucy came out of their dreams about the five-dollar gold piece. "Hi, Mr. Silverthorne," they said.

"What in all git-out were you all a-doing just now out there in front of the store? The way you were jumping about and a-carrying on, it looked like a swarm of bees had set on to you."

"Oh, my frogs got away," explained Chris. "We were trying to catch 'em."

"So that was it." Mr. Silverthorne thought a moment. "But say," he said, "didn't I see you grab that young fellow by the necktie? Now what did you do that for?" He peered at Chris, full of curiosity.

Chris looked a little ashamed. "He laughed at me," he said. "The man hollered out that old rhyme, *Way down yonder in Pasquotank, where the bullfrogs jump from bank to bank*. I'm mighty tired of hearing that. When the boy busted out laughing, it just naturally made me mad."

"Son," said Mr. Silverthorne, fishing into his pants' pocket and bringing up a bright nickel watch, "here. Take my watch! It's a present for ye. All my life I've wanted to take a poke at one of those smart alecks that come around hollering out that old rhyme. I consider you've done it for me. Take this-here watch and enjoy it."

"Do you mean it?" Chris exclaimed in surprise.

"I sure do. Here it is." Mr. Silverthorne clambered out of the cabin and handed the watch over the side of his boat. "It don't work," he said. "I dropped it overboard one time and the salt water rusted the insides, but it looks all right, just like new," he said.

"Gee, thanks, Mr. Silverthorne," Chris said happily. "I've always wanted a watch."

He looked at the watch with delight, then proudly put it into his pocket.

2. The Search for a Song

As THEY ROWED homeward from Mr. Midgett's store, Chris and Lucy were too excited to keep their boat headed in the right direction. It kept bumping its nose into the shore.

"Think what I could buy with five dollars!" exclaimed Chris. "I could buy that pair of cowboy boots."

"I could buy that furniture for Mrs. La Tour."

"Gee, I wish we could win that contest!" cried Chris. "Even if you took half the five dollars, and I the other half, it would be all right. It wouldn't take so *very* long to earn the rest."

"Papa knows a lot of good songs," said Lucy. "Maybe he could tell us one that would win."

"We'll ask him as soon as we get home!" Chris agreed.

They pulled hard on the oars. The little boat shot around the curves between the bulrushes. The cattails wagged as *Skeeter* sped along the canal. At last it reached its landing in a small ditch behind the barn.

Papa was in the barn lot, cleaning the disks of his new harrow, banging on them with a stick to make the dirt fall off.

"What's up, children?" he asked, as they came running up full of excitement.

They told him about the Showboat and the song contest.

"We certainly do want to win that prize, Papa," Lucy said eagerly. "Do you know a good song we could sing?"

"Well, let me see," said Papa thoughtfully. "What sort of song should you sing for a contest like that? It ought to be a lively one, I think. People like to laugh and feel happy." He pondered a moment. "Here's one that people like around here."

He began to sing, tapping merrily on the disks of his harrow to keep time with the music.

CLEVELAND'S ELECTED

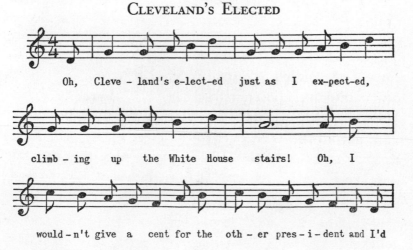

Oh, Cleve - land's e-lect-ed just as I ex-pect-ed,

climb - ing up the White House stairs! Oh, I

would - n't give a cent for the oth - er pres - i - dent and I'd

HERE COMES THE SHOWBOAT!

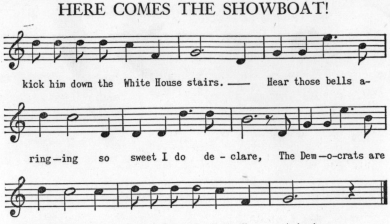

kick him down the White House stairs. —— Hear those bells a-

ring—ing so sweet I do de - clare, The Dem—o-crats are

sing - ing and climb—ing up the White House stairs!

"Oh, that's a fine one!" cried Chris and Lucy together.

There was a pause, then Lucy said: "But everybody knows it. Wouldn't it be better to sing a new song, Papa, something nobody else knows?"

"Well, that's a fact, it would," Papa agreed. "Your mother knows a lot of songs. Why don't you run into the house and ask her what to sing? I don't know any new ones."

Chris and Lucy ran to the house. They clattered up the back steps, through the kitchen, where Aunt Selina was bustling about, and into the parlor where Mama sat reading a magazine.

"Oh, Mama!" they cried. "The Showboat is coming next week and they're having a song contest. We want to win it. Can you tell us a song to sing?"

Mama was very interested.

"Let me see," she said, putting her finger to her chin.

She got up and went over to the great square piano. She sat down and played some sad-sounding chords. Then she sang *The Ballad of the Frozen Girl*. It was very long and sad. As she struck the last chord she turned on the piano stool.

"Do you think that might do?" she asked.

Mama sang The Ballad of the Frozen Girl.

Chris and Lucy felt dismal. The song had made them feel like crying.

"Why, Mama, it's a beautiful song," Lucy said, "but I think it's a little too sad. Papa says we should have something lively and merry to make people feel gay."

"Perhaps you had," Mama said. "Why don't you ask Aunt Selina what to sing? She's got a different song for everything she does. When she stirs a cake she sings a lively one. When she rolls dough she sings a slow one. She just moans something when she washes dishes. Oh, she's got a song for everything. Surely she should be able to think up a good one for you!"

Chris and Lucy ran hopefully into the kitchen. Aunt Selina was making scuppernong jelly. A basket full of the sweet white grapes that grow everywhere in the Carolina low country sat on the floor. More were boiling away in a big pot on the stove. The room was full of the delicious smell.

"Say, Aunt Selina," Chris said, sniffing with pleasure, "the Showboat's coming next week."

They told her all about the contest and how much they wanted to win it.

"Well, children, I sure would like to see you get that five-dollar gold piece," Aunt Selina said heartily. "Let me see what's the very best song I know." She laid down her spoon and wrinkled her brow in thought. "Now how do you like this one?" She lifted her voice and began to sing.

"Steal away, steal away, steal away to Jesus!
Steal away, steal away home! I ain't got long to stay here.
My Lord, He calls me, He calls me in the thunder!
The trumpet sounds within-a my soul, I ain't got long
    to stay here."

"That certainly is a beautiful song, Aunt Selina," said Chris, after she had finished.

"It certainly is," agreed Lucy. "But—but—it's a sort of hymn, isn't it? A church song. Do you think it would be proper for the Showboat?"

"Well now, maybe it wouldn't," Aunt Selina said.

"Don't you know some other kind of song?" Chris and Lucy asked together.

"The members of our church aren't allowed to sing worldly songs," said Aunt Selina firmly, shaking her head. "All the songs I sing are spiritual songs."

Chris and Lucy looked disappointed.

"Uncle Benny knows a lot of worldly songs," said Aunt Selina helpfully. "Maybe he knows one that would be good for your contest."

"Is it a new song?" Lucy asked.

"Why yes, maybe he does," Chris said. "We'll go ask him. Thank you just the same, Aunt Selina."

"Thank you, Aunt Selina," echoed Lucy.

Uncle Benny lived in a little house on the bank of the lead canal. It was surrounded by a thicket of myrtle trees and was all covered over with wild honeysuckle vines. The children ran across the fields to find him.

"I'll bet Uncle Benny can make my watch run," Chris said, as they neared the house. "He can fix anything else that's broken—broken chairs, broken harness, broken clocks, broken china. I'm just sure he can fix my watch."

"Maybe he can," Lucy replied.

Uncle Benny was sitting on his doorstep weaving a feed basket of rushes and hickory splints.

"Heigh-oh there, children. What are you up to now?" he asked, smiling at them.

Chris and Lucy began to talk at the same moment, Lucy

explaining about the song contest, Chris telling about his watch.

"Hold on, hold on there!" Uncle Benny cried. "I haven't got but one pair of ears! What are *you* saying now?" He looked down at the watch Chris was holding out.

"I wanted to know if you could fix my watch," Chris said.

"If it's got works, I can fix it," Uncle Benny said positively. He took the watch and peered inside. "Uh-huh. Little touch of rheumatism. Snake oil's the thing for this."

He put his basketry aside, went into the house, and returned with a small bottle.

"This is what I use when I got the rheumatism. If it can limber up my old rusty joints, it surely ought to make this watch go."

He let a few drops of snake oil fall into the watch, then picked at the works a little with a long needle.

"Scrape off a little rust here and a little rust there," he said. "Now I bet my best feather bed it goes right off to ticking."

He gave the watch a shake and held it up to his ear.

"Uh-huh!" He smiled with delight as he held it to Chris's ear. A loud ticktock could be heard from the watch.

"Oh, thank you, Uncle Benny!" Chris cried joyfully.

"Now don't you go showing it to whoever gave it to you," Uncle Benny admonished. "They'll surely try to take it back again."

"No, sir, Uncle Benny, I sure won't," promised Chris.

"Now what was that *you* were trying to tell me just now?" Uncle Benny asked, turning to Lucy.

She told him about the song contest on the Showboat.

"We want a nice lively song that'll be sure to win the prize," she concluded.

"Sing us the very best song that you know," Chris said.

"Well now, let me get my box. Can't sing much without my box."

Uncle Benny went into the house and returned with a battered guitar. Propping his chair back against the wall, he began to pick some merry chords, and to sing.

OLD AUNT DINAH

Old aunt Di-nah went to go to bed, She raised up the win-dow and poked out her head, A snow-ball hit her in the eye-ball, bim! look-a here chill-un don't you do that a-gain!

When he finished, the children laughed with delight.

"That's the best yet, don't you think so, Lucy?" asked Chris.

Lucy looked doubtful. "Is it a new song, Uncle Benny?" she asked.

"Lawsy no, child," he replied. "I used to sing that song to your papa when he was a little boy. I been singing that to children goin' on fifty years."

"We wanted a new song, Uncle Benny," Lucy explained. "Don't you know any new songs?"

"Lawsy no, honey," the old man said. "All my songs have come down to me from way back yonder in old times. I sure am sorry."

"Well, thank you anyway, Uncle Benny," Chris said.

As they walked slowly back to the house the children felt very discouraged.

"If you keep picking so many faults we'll never find a song," Chris said.

"But there's no use to sing one that won't win," Lucy answered. "If we sing the same old songs that people have heard over and over again, ever since they were born, they'll be bored and we won't get any prize. And suppose somebody else decided to sing the same one we did? Then we'd be sure to lose. We ought to have a lively song and a new one, that people haven't heard before."

They walked along feeling quite disheartened.

"I wonder what we could do now," Lucy said dismally.

"We could go back to the kitchen and see if Aunt Selina has finished that scuppernong jelly," said Chris, brightening. "It certainly would be nice to have a taste of scuppernong jelly."

"That won't help us find a new song."

"There's nothing in the whole world better than scuppernong jelly," was all Chris said.

He began to run toward the kitchen. Lucy followed him.

"Have you found that song, children?" asked Aunt Selina, as they entered the kitchen.

"No, we haven't," Chris said. "We thought we'd just come back to have a bit of jelly if you've got any to spare."

'I've saved this out just for you," Aunt Selina told them.

She set out a bowlful of quivering golden jelly. The children sat down and began to spread it on halves of biscuits.

"Nobody knows any new songs," mourned Lucy, as she bit into her treat. "What we need is a new song, a lively song. One that nobody's heard before."

"Listen!" said Aunt Selina. "The only way you're going to get a new song, a song that nobody's heard before, is to make one up for yourself."

"Make one up!" exclaimed Lucy. "Why, we couldn't!"

"How come you couldn't?" inquired Aunt Selina.

"I wouldn't know how to begin. Would you, Chris?"

"I sure wouldn't," said Chris, with his mouth full of jelly. "I never heard of anybody's making up a song."

"Lawsy me, child. We colored folks are all the time making up songs."

"You are?" Lucy said, surprised.

"Sure we are. We make up spiritual songs when we're in the church-house. We make up working songs when we're working in the fields or on the roads. We make up blues when we're feeling sad. We're all the time making up songs."

"How do you go about it?" asked Lucy.

"Well, the first thing, I reckon, your heart's got to be full of something," Aunt Selina said. "If your heart's not full, you can't make any song."

"What do you mean by that?" asked Chris, reaching for another biscuit and spreading more jelly.

"I mean that you've got to feel so full of something that you haven't got room in your heart for all of it. It's got to spill out some way."

"Like jelly and biscuit?" asked Chris, laughing and cramming his mouth full.

"No, child. Like sadness or gladness or meaness or madness. It's like this. Maybe we folks are sitting in church. There we are, all together, and we're thinking about how hard life is. Somebody sings out, sorrowful-like, *I hangs down my head and cries!* The preacher cries out, *Jesus going to wipe my weeping eyes.* And there we've got a beginning of a song. You see? Or maybe we're out in the pea patch. We see a little rabbit eating our peas. He's a cute little feller but just the same we don't want him eating up our peas. Somebody starts to sing about it. *Rabbit in the pea patch picking out peas. Get away rabbit, get away, please.* And there we got the start of a different kind of song. And we go on from there. Somebody adds a line and then somebody else adds another, and pretty soon we've got a song."

"I see," said Lucy. "But what about the tune? Do you make up your own tunes?"

"Sometimes we put our words to tunes we've heard somewhere, and change it around to suit ourselves. Sometimes the tune just oozes up out of us from deep down somewhere. It just comes natural, I reckon."

"It sounds easy," said Lucy.

"But is it as easy as it sounds?" Chris asked. "I don't think any tune is going to ooze out of me."

"Well, you never can tell till you try," Lucy said.

"That sure was good jelly, Aunt Selina," Chris remarked. "Thank you ever so much."

For several days Chris and Lucy waited hopefully for a song to spill out of their hearts but nothing happened. No tunes oozed up. They cudgeled their brains, but not an idea came to them. And the contest night was only a little more than a week away! At last, in despair, they went back to Aunt Selina.

"Our hearts don't seem to be full of anything," Lucy said to her in a worried voice. "Anyway, nothing seems to spill over. We can't get even a smidgen of an idea for a song. What can we do?"

Aunt Selina carefully turned a fish that she was frying for supper. Then she looked at them, frowning thoughtfully. After a moment she came close and bent over them.

"Listen!" she whispered mysteriously, looking all around to make sure no one was about. "I'll tell you something. Don't tell anybody what I say, you hear me?" She held up a warning finger.

"No, no, we won't tell, honest!" Chris and Lucy whispered.

"Go down to Devil Hole Swamp where the conjure man lives and get him to make you a voodoo charm."

Lucy took a backward step. Her eyes grew as round as onions.

"What's a voodoo charm, Aunt Selina?" Chris asked. "What will that do?"

"It'll bring you good luck. It'll put a song in your mind— just like that!" Aunt Selina snapped her fingers to show how quickly it would happen.

"It will?"

"Why sure it will. The conjure man can make all kinds of charms. Listen! Last month old Uncle Candy Jones lost his cow. He looked all over the fields and the swamps and everywhere. He had done lost hope of finding that cow. And so he went to the conjure man and got a charm, and what you reckon! Before he can say *Jack Robinson*, there was that cow right there in the conjure man's back yard! And listen! You know old Miss Lizzie Smith? She's all shriveled up so she can't even walk. Well, the conjure man made her that way. Somebody got mad with her and got the conjure man to put a spell on her. She began to shrivel and shrink and there she is now like an old dried-up potato. Oh, I tell you, the conjure man can do all kinds of voodoo, the good kind and the bad kind."

41

"Oh me, suppose he gave us the wrong kind by mistake?" said Lucy.

"He's not going to make any mistake like that," Aunt Selina reassured her.

"You know the conjure man, Aunt Selina, and we don't," Lucy said. "Why don't you go down and ask him for us?"

"Lawsy no, honey, not me!"

"Why not?" Lucy persisted.

"I'd just rather not, that's all," Aunt Selina said firmly.

"Devil Hole Swamp," Lucy said thoughtfully. "Gee, I think I'd be scared to go down there. Wouldn't you be scared, Chris?"

"Shucks, no," replied Chris. "I wouldn't be scared."

"That Devil Hole Swamp is a mighty gloomy-looking place," Lucy reflected.

"Oh, it's nothing to be afraid of," Chris said carelessly.

"Do you think we ought to try it?" asked Lucy.

"Sure, why not? If this conjure man can make us think up a song, why it's a cinch!" Chris declared.

"Well, if you're willing to try it, I am too," Lucy said stoutly. "When shall we go?"

"Let's go right after lunch," Chris decided.

3. The Conjure Man

"Do you think we can get there and back before dark?" Chris asked, as they were getting ready to make their visit to the conjure man. "You know Mama doesn't like for us to be gone after dark."

"Why of course," said Lucy positively. "It isn't very far, a mile or two, that's all."

"We can't get there in our boat," Chris said. "The canal doesn't go that way."

"It's a long way to walk," Lucy added.

"We'll hitch Zero to the cart," Chris decided. "He'll take us there in no time."

"You never can tell what Zero'll do," Lucy objected. "He might run away and throw us into the swamp."

"Don't dawdle on the swamp road," Aunt Selina said.

"Why he wouldn't run away," Chris argued. "He's as gentle as a lamb."

Aunt Selina appeared at the back door and beckoned to them mysteriously. They ran to see what she wanted.

"You better take the conjure man a little present," she whispered. "That puts him in a good humor."

"A present?" asked Chris. "What kind of present?"

"Well, he likes collard greens mighty well. You could take him a few heads of collard greens."

"What I want to know is," demanded Chris, "if he's a conjure man and can make magic, why doesn't he just make some collard greens appear when he wants 'em?"

44

"Maybe that's what he's doing, honey," Aunt Selina replied. "Maybe that's how come you're going down there. Maybe he's made a conjure to get him some collard greens."

Lucy and Chris looked at each other a little startled. The thought of being drawn down to the swamp by conjure magic made them feel very queer.

Zero started off at a lively trot.

"Well, we certainly can take him some collard greens," was all Lucy said. "There are plenty of collards in the garden."

"We'll get some right now," Chris agreed.

"Now, don't you dawdle on that swamp road," Aunt Selina shook a warning finger at them. "Soon as you get your voodoo charm you turn right 'round and come home fast as your feet can bring you."

"We sure will, Aunt Selina," Lucy and Chris promised together, as they set off at a trot for the vegetable garden.

They pulled up four heads of collard greens and put them carefully into the calf cart. Then Chris caught Zero and began to hitch him to the cart. As he was buckling the harness, Lucy had a sudden inspiration.

"I think I'll take Mrs. La Tour," she said. "She could wear her new blue linen traveling suit."

"That tiresome old doll!" exclaimed Chris. "She'll just be in the way."

"She would *not* be in the way," Lucy defended Mrs. La Tour. "I'll take care of her myself. I could pack her suitcase. It would be a fine chance for her to see a little something of the world."

"Well, all right then, go get her ready," grumbled Chris. He looked at his watch importantly. "But don't take too long about it. It's already—let me see, fifteen minutes past two."

Lucy ran to the house and into the playroom, where Mrs. La Tour lived in a large dollhouse that Lucy herself had made of some orange crates. She hurriedly dressed her in her new blue linen, combed her beautiful real blonde curls, and pinned on her stylish blue hat. Then she packed Mrs. La Tour's many dresses and underclothes and coats and sweaters and hats into a small doll's suitcase.

"Now we're all ready!" she said to Mrs. La Tour. "We're going on a long journey and I do hope you're going to enjoy it."

Mrs. La Tour lowered her eyes in a very worldly way, as if to say that traveling to her was just a bore. They hurried downstairs to the back door, where Chris was waiting with Zero and the cart.

"You certainly took long enough," he observed, taking his watch out of his pocket and examining it carefully. "It's thirty-two minutes after two o'clock."

"Oh, that's not very late," said Lucy. "We've got all afternoon."

46

She climbed up and settled herself in the cart.

"Get along there, Zero!" Chris cried, slapping the calf with the reins.

Zero started off at a lively trot. They rumbled over the bridge that spanned the canal in front of the house and started along the dusty country road.

It was a beautiful day. White clouds floated across the blue sky. Birds chirped in the trees along the roadside, and once they saw a squirrel sitting high up on the limb of a hickory tree, busily cracking nuts. Chris sat holding the reins, feeling very proud that his calf was behaving so well. Lucy sat beside him, holding Mrs. La Tour carefully so that she might have a good view of the scenery.

"This is fun, isn't it?" she asked. "We certainly were silly to be afraid."

"I wasn't afraid," Chris replied. "It was you."

They wheeled along. As they passed by a rambling old gray house with dormer windows, a little girl waved to them from the porch.

"Hey, Mittie Belle! Want to go?" called Lucy.

"Can't go, got to mind Miss Mamie's baby. Always got to mind the baby!" She held up the golden-haired child for them to see. "Come see me when you get back and we'll play dolls."

"All right," promised Lucy. "Good-by," she waved gaily.

For about half a mile the calf trotted smartly along. Then they came to the place where a narrow, rough road led off through the cypress swamp.

"Whoa!" Chris called, and pulled in the reins. "Here's where we turn."

Lucy peered doubtfully down the gloomy swamp road. On either side lay black silent pools of water. Towering

47

cypress trees grew up from them, their gloomy foliage high above shutting out all sunlight. Beards of long gray moss hung everywhere from all the limbs, from all the bushes. The road was like an enbankment leading between two dark lakes. A few scrawny water bushes and some purplish-red snakeflowers grew along its edge.

"I—I wonder if we ought to go," Lucy quavered.

"Why not?" exclaimed Chris in surprise.

"Mama might miss us."

"You know we go off any time we like and stay till night. Mama doesn't care."

"Well," Lucy began, "this poor little calf. Do you think he can stand such a long trip? Do you think it's good for him? We've got a heavy load, an awful heavy load, for such a little calf. With all these collards and Mrs. La Tour and all her clothes."

"Shucks, he doesn't even feel it," Chris answered.

At this moment a lean black cat crept silently across the road in front of them.

"Say, that means bad luck!" cried Lucy. She stared after the cat in dismay. "Aunt Selina says if a black cat crosses your path when you start out on a trip, you'd better turn around and go on back home."

"Shucks, it's only Miss Mamie's old tom, out hunting field mice," Chris said. "What harm can that do? Get along there!" he shouted at the calf.

Zero struck up a lazy trot.

"Oh, me!" groaned Lucy.

The road was full of holes. The children jostled and jounced along. Mosquitoes swarmed up from the stagnant water and settled on their arms and legs. They buzzed about Zero's head. The calf kicked and snorted.

"We're going to be eaten alive!" cried Lucy, slapping

her neck. "We're going to catch malaria with all these mosquitoes."

"You're making a mountain out of a molehill," Chris said scornfully. "Get out and break some bushes and keep 'em off."

He stopped the calf and Lucy got out and broke some great branches from a water bush. She climbed in again and beat the branches about their shoulders and legs, and across the calf's back.

"Uncle Benny told me one time that the mosquitoes in this swamp were so big that any one of them could whip a dog in a fair fight," Lucy said. "Now I can believe him."

"Two of 'em could fly away with a full-sized man," Chris agreed. "But you're doing pretty well with that bush. Just keep it up and we'll get there safe and sound."

They rumbled along. The way seemed endless. It got gloomier as they went on. They passed a ruined sawmill. Its great rusted boiler and machinery, all overgrown with vines and weeds, looked like hidden, crouching monsters.

The children were beginning to despair of finding the conjure man's house, when through the scrawny branches of the cypress trees they spied a tumble-down shanty.

"Whoa, there!" Chris pulled on the reins. "Do you think that could be the conjure man's house?"

"It must be. Aunt Selina said there was only one house down this way."

They peered at the dilapidated cabin. It stood on a small island in the swamp, connected to the road by an old rotten bridge. Its roof was sagging. Its broken windowpanes were stuffed with old rags. In the front yard a smouldering fire burned underneath a large black pot.

"There's it for sure," Lucy said, her eyes popping. "There's his conjure pot."

Chris stared at the pot. "What do they put in a conjure pot, anyhow?" he asked.

"Why all kinds of horrible things," Lucy replied. "Snakes' legs and moles' eyes and frogs' tails, and things like that. And they stew them all up with graveyard dirt."

"But snakes haven't got legs and moles haven't got eyes and frogs haven't got tails," Chris objected.

"Aunt Selina says they have," Lucy retorted. "We can't see 'em but the conjure man can."

"Oh, I see." Chris eyed the smoking pot. After a pause he said: "If we're going, I guess we'd better go. Let's tie Zero right here. If we tried to get the cart across that bridge it might break through."

Chris got out and tied the calf to the trunk of a large water bush. Lucy got out too, looking fearfully around in the dismal twilight. Not a soul was in sight. Not a sound was to be heard. She propped Mrs. La Tour carefully in the bottom of the cart.

"You'd better stay here," she said. "I don't want to have any voodoo spell cast on you. I'd hate to have you shrink and shrivel up." Mrs. La Tour popped her eyes wide open.

The children gathered up the collard greens and tiptoed across the bridge. A weedy path led past the smoking pot to the cabin door.

They followed it hesitantly.

"Do you think it's all right to go in like this, without any invitation, while the conjure pot is going?" Lucy asked, hanging back. "Maybe the conjure man wouldn't like it. Maybe he'd make a bad voodoo against us. I'd hate to shrivel and shrink like that woman Aunt Selina told us about."

Just then she stumbled over something lying across the path. Looking down, she drew back in terror. Two legs and

He stuffed branches under the great black pot.

a pair of feet lay across the way. The body was hidden by bushes.

"What's this? Somebody dead?" she exclaimed.

"My gosh! It looks like it!" Even Chris looked frightened.

"Somebody the conjure man made a voodoo against," gasped Lucy. "We'd better go home."

"Maybe we'd better," Chris agreed.

Then the legs moved. A head appeared out of the bushes and a sleepy-looking old Negro sat up on the path. For a moment both Chris and Lucy stood frozen in their tracks, staring at the wrinkled old face. Then they were struck by something familiar.

"Why, it's Uncle Joe, who comes to shuck corn every fall," Lucy said.

"Hello, Uncle Joe," said Chris.

"For the land's sakes!" the old man exclaimed. "What

are you children doing way down here in the swamp?"

"Why, we came to see the conjure man," Lucy answered. "We thought this was his house. Do you know where he lives?"

"He lives right here," said Uncle Joe. "I'm the conjure man."

"You are," Lucy said, crestfallen.

It was rather disappointing to find this harmless, friendly old man to be the conjure man.

"Is that your conjure pot?" she asked hopefully, pointing to the great black pot over the smouldering fire.

"Conjure pot? Lawsy me, I clean forgot that pot!" Uncle Joe's voice was worried. "Lawsy no, child, that's my old lady's washpot. She's boiling the clothes in there. She sent me out here to watch and make sure the fire doesn't go out. I declare, I must have fallen asleep. I've got to get some wood on that fire. Look's like it's about to go out, doesn't it? My old woman will quarrel something awful if I let this fire go out."

He scurried about, picking up dead branches and twigs and stuffing them under the pot. When the fire was blazing merrily, he came back to the path where the children stood waiting.

"We want to get a good-luck charm, Uncle Joe," Lucy said. "We brought you these collard greens."

Uncle Joe took the greens. "Well, I declare. I was thinking only this morning that I sure wished I had a good mess of collard greens to go with my fried fish. Sure do thank you. You say you want a good-luck charm?"

"Yes, Uncle Joe. You see, they're having a song contest on the Showboat and we want to win it," explained Chris. "There's a five-dollar prize."

"Five dollars! Gosh!" Uncle Joe shook his head in amaze-

52

"Wear this and Good Luck is going to follow you."

ment. "Well, I sure have to find you the best charm I've got. Five dollars! Whooey!" He hobbled into the little cabin and came out with a large rusty horseshoe that he presented to Chris.

"You put this up over your bed at night," he said, "pointed up, so the luck won't spill out, and I guarantee you'll get that five-dollar prize."

"Oh, thank you, Uncle Joe," said Chris gratefully.

"And look, here's what I've got for you," Uncle Joe said to Lucy.

Taking a small tin box from his pocket, he opened it and took out a large lump of yellowish powder. He dropped it into a small piece of cloth and tied the corners together.

"Gee, Uncle Joe! What's that stuff? It smells *awful*," said Lucy.

"It's asafetida, child. It's a kind of medicine. I reckon it's the very worst-smelling thing in the whole world. But don't pay any attention to that. That's what makes it good voodoo. It smells so bad it keeps all the bad luck away."

"Seems to me it would keep all the good luck away too," said Chris.

"No, honey," Uncle Joe said, "that's not the way it works." He fastened the asafetida onto a string and tied it around Lucy's neck. "Now, honey, you just wear this—so. And Good Luck is going to follow you everywhere you go."

"Phew! She ought to be able to tell where I am, all right," said Lucy, holding her nose. "This is one bad smell, sure enough, but thank you just the same, Uncle Joe. If we win that song contest, I don't care how bad it smells." She turned to Chris. "Do you think we ought to go home now? You know what Aunt Selina told us."

Chris looked at his watch.

"It's ten minutes past four," he said. "Yep. Reckon it's time to go."

They thanked Uncle Joe for their good-luck charms and told him good-by.

When they got back to the calf cart they found Mrs. La Tour waiting patiently. Zero was cropping the tops of the flag leaves and chewing contentedly. Chris untied him and the children climbed into the cart.

"Get along there!" cried Chris.

Zero merely reached for another bite of delicious greenery. "Hiya! Get along!" Chris shouted again, slapping the calf with the reins.

Zero stood happily munching. He did not move.

"Suppose he won't go home?" asked Lucy.

Down the dusky swamp road Zero flew.

"He's got to go! Gee up there!" Chris bawled, slapping Zero's sides again.

The calf took a few steps forward to a fresh clump of flags. He was having a nice treat and he had no intention of leaving it.

"Get out and lead him a little way," Lucy suggested. "Maybe that will get him in the notion to go."

Chris got out and pulled Zero away from his picnic lunch. He led him a few steps down the road, then climbed back into the cart.

"Now get along! It's getting late."

Zero trotted a few steps, then stopped for more refreshments. "We'll never get home this way," wailed Lucy.

Again Chris got out and pulled Zero along the road. Again the calf took a few lagging steps, only to pause again for another bite. And so it went, until the children were in despair.

"It's getting toward five o'clock," Chris said in a worried voice.

"It's almost suppertime," Lucy said in a dismayed tone.

It grew gloomier and gloomier in the swamp. Night would be falling soon. Strange noises began to sound. There were weird clickings and chitterings. The great bullfrogs began to bellow, *Jug-o-rum! Jug-o-rum!* Their voices sounded deep and threatening. The little frogs shrieked *Knee-deep! Knee-deep!*

Still Zero dawdled and lingered, nibbling at the flags and refusing to go more than a few steps at a time.

"Gee, we've got to get him out of here!" cried Lucy. "Twist his tail, Chris. That ought to make him go."

"Twist his tail?" Chris asked.

"Certainly. That's what they do to get a balky mule to go."

"All right. Here goes!" Chris grasped the calf's tail and twisted hard.

"Ba-a-a!" Zero leaped with pain and astonishment. "Ba-a-a!" he bawled with terror, and set off at a frantic gallop.

"Whoa! Whoa!" cried Chris. "This is too fast!"

Zero paid no attention. Down the dusky swamp road he flew. The children held on with all their might. The cart bounded and bounced. It threatened to turn over every moment.

"Stop him! Stop him!" shouted Lucy. "He's running away!"

"I can't stop him!" Chris howled, tugging and pulling on the reins. "He won't stop!"

"Oh, lawsy, there goes Mrs. La Tour's suitcase!"

Out the back went the little suitcase. It flew open and all Mrs. La Tour's dresses and petticoats and panties were scattered along the road.

"Oh, wait, wait!" begged Lucy. "There goes Mrs. La

With a loud splash the cart sank among the lily pads.

Tour's clothes. Her silk dress—everything. Wait! Wait!"
But Zero did not pause.

"Oh me! Oh me!" moaned Lucy, clasping her precious doll, lest she follow the suitcase, and holding on at the same time, as best she could, to the sides of the cart.

"We're coming to the main road," Chris yelled. "We're going to make the turn. Hold tight!"

"Oh, we're turning over!" screamed Lucy.

But the cart did not turn over. It tilted, skittered a moment on one wheel, then righted itself. They were on the main road and Zero stretched out for home. The children held on grimly as they flew like the wind. Dust streamed out behind like smoke.

As they galloped past Miss Mamie's house, Mittie Belle ran out and shouted after them.

"Hey!" she yelled. "Why don't you stop? Let's play dolls."

Lucy did not answer. It was all she could do to hold on. In a moment, Mittie Belle was far behind. Their own home came quickly into view.

"We're coming to the bridge!" Chris shouted. "I hope he makes it."

"Hold on to your good-luck horseshoe!" screeched Lucy.

On sped Zero. The bridge was not in his mind. Why bother with a bridge? There were quicker ways of crossing. He gathered himself for a leap. The children yelled in vain.

With one great bound, Zero jumped the canal. The cart did not make it. With a loud splash it sank among the lily pads, carrying Chris and Lucy and Mrs. La Tour with it.

Zero struggled to free himself from the cart. He kicked and lunged. The harness broke, but Chris clung to the reins and was dragged from the canal.

"Whoa! Whoa there!" Chris kept coughing and spitting out brown canal water. He stopped the calf at last.

"Help! Help!" Lucy scrambled up. She stood spouting water like a hippopotamus. It ran from her as from a rain-spout.

"Oh, where is Mrs. La Tour?" she cried. She spied her precious doll, luckily floating on the water, held up by her fancy petticoats.

"Her hair, her beautiful hair!" shrieked Lucy, as she rescued Mrs. La Tour from the water. "It's gone! She's baldheaded! The glue has melted, she's lost her hair! Oh, where's her hair?"

She looked about frantically. At last she saw it, a soggy mess, caught on the stem of a cattail.

"It will never be pretty and curly again!" cried Lucy.

She climbed out of the canal, carrying Mrs. La Tour, a great hole gaping in the middle of her skull.

"Look what's happened," she said to Chris, showing him the dreadful state of her doll. "This is terrible! And all her beautiful clothes!"

Chris jerked the calf's reins angrily. "It's all your fault!" he said to the animal.

Zero did not like such talk. He let fly with a swift kick. It hit Chris with a crack.

"Ouch!" Chris yelped. "He kicked me. What was that crash? I heard something break."

He put his hand into his pocket and brought out his watch. Wheels, springs and works fell out on the ground. The case was broken and bent.

"My watch is busted!" cried Chris. "This doggone calf has busted my watch!"

"You've still got your lucky horseshoe," Lucy said. "There it is, hanging on the side of the cart."

"Lucky horseshoe!" Chris looked about at the wreckage. "This doesn't look like good luck to me." He seized the horseshoe to heave it away.

"Wait! Wait!" Lucy cried. "Don't throw it away. This— this is just an accident. The voodoo won't begin to work until you put it up over your bed. Like Uncle Joe said, with the ends pointing up."

"Huh!" Chris rubbed the place where the calf had kicked him.

"Oh, mercy! What's happened?" Mama and Aunt Selina and Papa came running.

"Lawsy, lawsy me!" Aunt Selina clapped both hands to her face.

Papa stood laughing heartily. He said it was the worst wreck he had ever seen.

4. Asafetida

As THE CHILDREN took their places at the supper table the evening of the accident, Lucy hoped with all her heart that no one would smell the asafedita that still hung about her neck, underneath her dress. The wetting it had received had made it smell even worse than ever. She was not at all sure Mama would approve of it.

She was very hungry and looked at the food with pleasure. There was a large platter full of crabs caught fresh from the Pasquotank River and fried to a crisp golden brown. There was delicious wild asparagus stewed in milk, and a cut-glass dish full of spicy mustard pickles. Aunt Selina appeared immediately with a casserole full of piping-hot spoon bread, which she passed around. Everyone in turn dipped out a spoonful and spread it with butter. Mama poured old-fashioned yaupon tea from a large teapot and the cups were passed around.

Chris and Lucy always enjoyed the tea. They themselves had picked the yaupon leaves from the low green hedges that grew along the beaches. It was a favorite drink with Papa, too. As he sipped it, he sometimes liked to tell its story.

"Yaupon is good for the blood, children," he began.

Chris and Lucy looked up expectantly. They had heard it all before, but it still seemed interesting.

"Long ago," Papa continued, "the Hatteras Indians used to drink it as a tonic. They said it was good medicine and taught the white settlers to use it. Those old sea captains, Amidas and Barlow, sent out by Sir Walter Raleigh to explore this part of North Carolina, probably sipped some of this very same tea. That was away back in 1584. Later on, people around the coast used to make quite a lot of money picking the leaves and curing them and shipping them away. When I was a little boy—" Papa paused, sniffing the air. "What's that I smell?"

Mama sniffed too and frowned. "Something must be dead," she said. She looked over Lucy's shoulder toward the window. "Something must have died out in the field. Please close the window, Chris."

Lucy began to eat hurriedly.

"If you close the window, it might get worse," said Chris.

"No, I think not. Please go ahead and close it."

Chris got up and closed the window.

After a moment Mama said: "I believe you're right. It *is* worse. Open it again. It must be a mouse that's dead inside the woodwork."

"It smells like a rotten egg to me," said Papa. "Look in the egg basket, Chris. Maybe somebody has broken a bad egg."

Chris got up again. "No, sir, no egg broken," he said, shaking his head, and sat down again.

Lucy began to stuff in spoon bread and crab and asparagus as fast as she could swallow it. Something told her that she would not be able to finish her meal.

"My gracious! This is awful," Mama exclaimed. "What can it be?"

Papa laid down knife and fork and sniffed like a bird dog. "It smells something like burning sulphur," he said. "You remember the time we burned sulphur to fumigate the rooms after the children had scarlet fever. It smells something like that. Have you been fumigating?"

"No, of course not," Mama replied impatiently. "That's not it. I don't know what it can be. It seems to come from over that side where Lucy is sitting."

Cramming a large piece of crab into her mouth, Lucy got up. "Please excuse me, Mama," she said. "I've had enough. I think I'll go now." She cast a longing look at the food she had left on her plate.

"Are you sick?" Mama demanded.

"No, Mama, I don't think so. Just a little headache, maybe."

"It's this awful smell. I'm beginning to get a headache, too. We'll *have* to find it."

Lucy ran upstairs to her bedroom and quickly closed the door. She stood biting her lip and thinking hard. The smell of asafetida was with her wherever she went.

"When Mama comes up to see how I am feeling, she'll smell it again," she said to herself. "And this time she'll know it's me. She'll certainly make me throw it away."

"I hope you haven't got malaria," Mama said.

That would never do, Lucy felt. It would be the end of their hopes to win the song contest. What could she do?

"I'll get into bed and pile on a lot of covers so the smell will not come through," she thought.

She hurried out to the hall, where the winter covers were kept in a great chest packed between leaves of tobacco to keep the moths away. She was pleased to get the strong whiff of tobacco as she raised the lid.

"That's stronger than asafetida," she said to herself, as she dragged out the blankets. "It'll smother the smell—I hope!"

She put two pairs of double blankets on her bed, quickly undressed and crawled under the covers. The smell of asafetida mingled with the odor of tobacco and made a dreadful mixture. It was a warm summer night and the blankets were thick and woolly. Poor Lucy soon felt that she was beginning to melt away.

In a little while there was a light tap on the door.

"Come in," Lucy said faintly.

Mama entered.

"My goodness!" she exclaimed. "What have you got all those covers on for? Have you got a chill?"

"Well, I felt a little cold," Lucy replied.

"Oh, my gracious!" Mama cried in alarm. "I hope you haven't got a case of malaria. That's how it begins. A headache and then a chill and then the fever."

"No, Mama. I don't think that's it."

"I must call your father."

Mama went into the hall and called down the stairs. Papa came up. Lucy heard them whispering outside the door. She knew they were talking about malaria. It was an illness brought by mosquitoes from the swamp.

"I'll take a look at her," Lucy heard Papa say. "If she's got the symptoms, I'll call a doctor at once."

He came into the room. "How do you feel, Lucy?" Papa asked cheerily.

Chris was with him and stood at the foot of the bed. Papa sat down on the bed.

"It doesn't look like malaria," he said to Mama.

"I'm not sick, honest, Mama," Lucy said. "Maybe I got cold when I fell into the canal. I haven't got warm yet. I'll be all right in a little while, then I'll take the covers off."

Mama and Papa stood over her, looking puzzled and worried. Then, telling her good night, they went away. Chris stayed, still standing at the foot of the bed.

Lucy immediately sat up and threw off the covers. "I'm blistering," she said. "I'm burning up."

64

"What did you put all that stuff on the bed for?" Chris asked.

"Why, to keep the asafetida from smelling all over the room."

"Silly!" Chris said. "Why didn't you just lie down on your stomach? That would have kept the asafetida underneath you."

"I never thought of that!" Lucy exclaimed. She threw the blankets back over the foot of the bed. "What have you done with your horseshoe?" she asked.

"I've got it propped up over the head of my bed, like Uncle Joe said. I'll go on to bed now. And let me tell you I hope these charms will hurry up and work. If they don't, we're both going to get into a peck of trouble."

"I hope so too," Lucy said fervently.

Chris said good night and went into his own room.

After he had gone, Lucy sat up in bed, thinking over their trip to the conjure man. Poor Mrs. La Tour had got the worst of it. There she lay on the bureau, still a little soggy, the hole in the top of her head gaping horribly. Beside her was her blonde hair all straight and straggly.

"Dear Mrs. La Tour," Lucy murmured, "maybe I can mend you and make you new again."

She hopped out of bed, rummaged among her things, and brought out a pair of curling tongs that were used to curl her hair on very special occasions. She heated the tongs by holding them above the lamp. Then she applied them to Mrs. La Tour's wig.

"Just look!" Lucy cried happily to Mrs. La Tour, after she had finished. "Your hair is as beautiful and as curly as ever. Now we'll see if we can't paste it on your head again." She brought out a small gluepot and applied a liberal quantity to her doll's bald skull. Then she carefully put the wig in place. "Now just look at yourself!" she exclaimed, holding the doll up to the mirror. "You're as beautiful as ever!"

Mrs. La Tour fluttered her eyes with pleasure.

"And Monday, I promise you," Lucy went on, "I shall start on a whole new outfit for you—panties, petticoats, lots of beautiful new dresses. You'll be glad you lost the others, just wait and see!"

Mrs. La Tour's eyes flew wide open with delight.

At this moment there was a crash from the next room, then a loud outcry from Chris. Lucy ran to his door.

"Say, what's the matter?" she cried.

Chris was sitting on the floor, rubbing his head. "Something knocked me on the head," he explained. Bewildered, he picked up an object from the floor. "It was my lucky horseshoe. It knocked me on the head and almost brained me." Leaping up angrily, he strode to the window and pitched it out. "I don't want anything more to do with that thing," he said.

"Oh, me!" Lucy cried in despair. "All we've got to depend on now is the asafetida." She ran back to her room and went to bed.

Lucy woke the next morning and blinked sleepily. The sun was shining brightly. What a beautiful day! But surely, the air was not so fresh as usual. No indeed, it was not! There was a dreadful odor somewhere.

"Phew! What can it be!" she exclaimed, sitting up in bed. Then she remembered. Asafetida!

"Gee whiz! I'd better get up and get out in the air before Mama comes in," she thought.

She jumped out of bed, flung on her clothes and ran outdoors. In the dewy morning air the asafetida was not so noticeable. Chris was in the corner of the yard, busily

"I don't smell anything," said Lucy quickly.

milking the cow. Lucy crossed the yard to speak to him.

"Good morning, how's your head?" she asked.

"It's sore." Chris felt gingerly of a lump that had swelled to the size of a goose egg.

"I'm worried about breakfast," said Lucy.

"Breakfast?"

"Just as soon as I sit down to the table," Lucy said, "they'll begin to smell again and this time they'll probably find out it's me."

HERE COMES THE SHOWBOAT!

Chris stopped milking and sat pondering. "Why don't you get Aunt Selina to give you your breakfast now?" he said at last.

"I could try it," Lucy agreed hopefully.

"You'd better hurry," he urged her. "It's nearly breakfast time."

"Oh, me," sighed Lucy. "You certainly do have to work hard to have good luck."

She ran along to the kitchen and peered through the screen door.

"Oh, Aunt Selina," she called. "I'm so hungry. Couldn't I have my breakfast now?"

Aunt Selina was busy cutting up a chicken. It was Sunday and she was getting the dinner early so that she could go to church.

"Listen here, I haven't got time to be serving two breakfasts," she said. "Breakfast is all ready on the stove. If you want to get yours now, you can come and get it."

Quickly Lucy darted in, got a plate, knife and fork from the cupboard, and went to the stove. She helped herself to the corn bread, selected a piece of fried ham from the pan, and dipped up a large spoonful of ham gravy and poured it on the corn bread.

Aunt Selina turned around as she was leaving. "Seems to me like I smell something," she remarked in a puzzled voice. "What's that bad smell?"

"I don't smell anything," said Lucy quickly, hurrying out.

As she sat outside on the flat top of the great brick water cistern, eating her breakfast, it seemed to her that everything tasted of asafetida.

"And I do like ham gravy and corn bread," she sighed dismally. "Six more days before the Showboat comes. I don't know how I'm going to keep this up."

ASAFETIDA

Soon it was time to get ready for church. Lucy climbed the stairs to her room. She wished she did not have to go. Suppose the smell of asafetida began to float through the church. She wondered what would happen. If only she had stayed in bed this morning and pretended to be sick! But it was too late now.

"Perhaps if I put lots of clothes on top of the asafetida the smell won't get out," she said to herself.

She got out six pantywaists and five ruffled petticoats. She hung the asafetida next to her skin and put on all the pantywaists and all the petticoats. They made her look tubby. Lucy could hardly recognize herself in the mirror, she had become so fat. And her lovely embroidered dress would hardly button around her.

"But if they keep the smell in," she thought, "I don't care if I do look like a pork barrel."

As she was tying her pink taffeta sash about her waist, Chris came into the room.

"How do I look?" asked Lucy.

Chris gazed at her in amazement. "What's happened to you?" he cried. "You look like a fattening pig. You weren't this fat a little while ago!"

"I put a lot of clothes on top of that asafetida," she explained, "so people won't smell it in church."

The family was a little late getting started, and in the hurry and scurry of getting off Mama did not notice anything unusual about Lucy. As they rode along to church in the family surrey, a cool, salt breeze blew from the river. It ruffled the fringe around the top of the surrey and blew away the smell of asafetida. Lucy began to feel cheerful. Perhaps there would be a breeze through the church.

The horses clopped along. At last they came upon the little white steepled Methodist church set back in the pine

69

woods. They got out and tied the horse in the shade of a pine tree. All their friends and neighbors were trooping into the wide double doors. Papa, Mama, Lucy and Chris followed them and sat in a pew very near the pulpit.

It was a warm day. Sunshine sifted through the blinds that shaded the tall windows. Outside, in the graveyard that surrounded the church, gardenia bushes grew head high. They were white with blossoms and the sweet smell of the flowers drifted into the open windows and filled the church with their scent.

The preacher began his sermon.

"I will take as my text this morning," he said, "the words of Jesus, *Suffer little children, and forbid them not, to come unto me: for such is the kingdom of heaven.*"

It was sultry inside the church. The surrounding woods shut away the breeze. Inside her six pantywaists and five petticoats Lucy grew warmer and warmer. The asafetida next to her skin began to melt with the heat. It steamed like a teakettle.

Slowly but surely a strange and awful odor began to mingle with the sweet smell of gardenias. It overcame the gardenias. People fanned harder and looked about uneasily. Those sitting near the Gale family put their handkerchiefs to their noses. The preacher paused in his sermon once or twice and drew in his breath.

"It's that same smell that was in the dining room last night!" Mama whispered to Papa. She held her violet-perfumed handkerchief in front of her nose and breathed through it.

Lucy glanced at Chris, her eyes popping, as if to say, "I'm afraid it's coming now."

At last the preacher stopped speaking. He looked about the congregation.

Chris and Lucy walked down the long aisle.

"I've read in the Bible," he said, "that the fires down below are made of burning sulphur. If it's true, as the Bible says, then it seems to me we're all in danger of hell fire, for I do believe I smell sulphur burning somewhere and that mighty close by."

There was the barest crinkle of a smile about his eyes.

71

"Does anybody know of anything else that might be causing that smell?" he asked.

Everybody looked at everybody else. Then a deacon who was sitting just next to the Gales spoke up.

"It might be a skunk underneath the church," he suggested.

The people of the congregation shook their heads. They knew what a skunk smelled like.

Then, toward the back of the church, a little girl arose. It was Mittie Belle, who had been brought along to take Miss Mamie's baby out if it began to cry.

"I know what it is, Reverend," she said. "It's not sulphur, and it's not any skunk. Somebody's got on a voodoo charm. It's an asafetida charm. I had one myself one time. The conjure man gave it to me. So I know what it is." She sat down, full of importance.

All over the church people began to titter. The preacher looked shocked.

"If anyone has on a voodoo charm," he said sternly, "I will ask them to please leave the church."

Mama looked angrily from Chris to Lucy. "It's one of you!" she whispered. "Whichever one it is, get up this minute and go outside!"

Lucy wished sincerely that a hole would open up in the floor and let her drop out of sight. Slowly she got up. Her face flushed a bright pink. To her surprise, Chris got up too.

As they walked down the long aisle, people looked at them and put their hands over their mouths, trying not to laugh out loud. That walk to the door seemed to Lucy the longest she had ever taken. How happy she was to get outside where there were only horses to stare at her!

"Why did you come, too?" she asked Chris.

"I've got an idea for our song!" Lucy cried.

"Well, it was my fault as well as yours," said Chris. "I thought I might as well take part of the blame."

They climbed into the carriage and sat down on the back seat.

"I think Mama's going to punish us," said Lucy miserably.

Chris nodded wretchedly.

"I wish we hadn't ever gone to the conjure man," said Lucy. "We've had nothing but bad luck since we went. I'm going to throw this thing away." She brought out the asafetida and flung it into the bushes.

73

"Have you got any idea for a song, any at all?" asked Chris.

"No, not even a smidgen."

The children were dismally quiet for a while. They slapped a mosquito or two. The horse stamped and switched at horseflies.

"If Aunt Selina told the truth about how to make up a song," Lucy said, "now's the time it ought to spill. She said your heart had to be so full of something that there wasn't room for all of it. Well, my heart's full all right. I never felt so miserable in all my life. Everybody laughing at us like that! I never want to come to church again as long as I live!"

"I don't either," agreed Chris.

"And that preacher! He said *Suffer little children to come unto me*. And then he made us go out. I reckon it's this way—Suffer little children to come unto me unless they're wearing asafetida!" said Lucy bitterly.

"You made a rhyme then," remarked Chris.

Lucy said nothing. She sat thinking of the rhyme, drooping dismally, listening to the July flies buzzing in the trees. Then suddenly she straightened up.

"Chris!" she cried. "I believe I've got an idea for our song!"

"You have!" exclaimed Chris. "What is it?"

During the next hour, while the preacher's voice rose and fell inside the church, Chris and Lucy sat making up verses for their song. They were full of excitement. All their troubles were forgotten.

The preaching was over at last and everybody poured out of the double doors. As soon as they were outside of the church, people began to laugh heartily, all except Mama and Papa. They looked very grim, and they came directly

74

to the carriage. They were surprised to see both Chris and Lucy looking so happy.

Papa untied the horse and they drove quickly away.

"Whatever made you do such a thing!" Mama exclaimed, as soon as they were out of the churchyard. "Voodoo is no earthly good for anything. It's just an old superstition. Scarcely anybody believes in such things any more. And asafetida of all things! Why you almost smoked everybody out of the church. You are to go to your rooms as soon as you've had your dinner and stay there until suppertime. And no reading of books, either!"

"Yes, Mama," said Chris and Lucy meekly.

The children never spent a busier afternoon than that Sunday shut up in their rooms. With pencil and paper they sat writing down words for their song.

Sometimes Lucy called through the door to Chris, "What rhymes with *do?*" and Chris shouted back, "*Flew* and *shoe* and *who*."

The time seemed to fly. When Mama came to let them out at suppertime, she found them pleased and excited.

Their song was completed.

5. The Showboat

EARLY ON MONDAY MORNING Chris and Lucy dashed across the yard and through the myrtle thicket to Uncle Benny's house. Lucy had a paper on which the words of their song were written down. They found the old man inside, finishing up his breakfast of fried pork with hoecake and molasses. The children hovered about him.

"Say, Uncle Benny, we want you to think up a tune for our song."

"Your song?" asked the old man, wiping his mouth on his sleeve. "What song?"

"Why, the one for the contest," Chris explained. "We've written one and we want a tune to fit it. A nice lively tune!"

Uncle Benny took his guitar from Chris.

"Goodness gracious sake's alive!" Uncle Benny exclaimed. "You ought to have picked your tune first and then made your words to fit the tune. You've gone about it hind part before."

"We have?" Lucy and Chris exclaimed together in dismay.

"Sure have, but anyhow we'll try and see what we can do about it."

Uncle Benny took his guitar from Chris and tuned it a little.

"How's this?" he asked, as he strummed a few chords. "Maybe this tune will fit your song." With a merry wink he began to sing:

> *"Mammy had a chicken, crowed just 'fore day*
> *'Long came a weasel and stole that chicken away,*
> *Row rye row, row rye row, row rye row,*
> *Row that boat ashore."*

"No, no," said Lucy, as he ended the song. "That won't fit."

"Well, then, here's another one." Uncle Benny plucked some more chords. "See will this do:

> *"I met a 'possum on the road,*
> *I asked him where was he gwine;*
> *He said it was his business*
> *And wasn't none of mine!"*

"No, that won't do either." Chris shook his head.

"Well, let me see now, what else do I know?" Uncle Benny scratched his head thoughtfully, then plunked a few chords and sang another song. It did not fit. He tried another and another and another. Nothing fitted Chris and Lucy's song.

"That's all the songs I know," he said at last. "It just looks like you'll have to make up one yourselves."

"We can't make up a tune, Uncle Benny!" Lucy protested, while Chris nodded agreement. "We've thought and thought."

"Why, honey, you don't think, you just listen if you want to make up a tune," Uncle Benny replied. "Everything's got music in it, if you listen. Now trim your ears when I go outdoors to give the rest of my hoecake to the dog, and see if you can hear any music."

Chris and Lucy looked puzzled as the old man took the remains of his breakfast, opened the door and went outside.

"Now what did you hear?" he demanded when he came back.

"Didn't hear anything," Chris stated positively.

"Well, nothing but the door squeaking," added Lucy.

"Uh-huh!" exclaimed Uncle Benny. "So you heard the door squeak. What did it say?"

Lucy frowned with concentration. "When it opened it said—"

"And when it shut?" questioned Uncle Benny.

Lucy tried the door again and listened carefully. "It sort of goes down the scale, like this—"

"Of course it does," agreed Uncle Benny. "And that's enough to begin on. Just start out like the door did—this way." He picked up his guitar and strummed it a little, while he hummed the tune the door had made. "Then if you don't know what to sing next, just *tramp, tramp, tramp* a little with the same note."

"You've seen children all lined up to march in a parade.

Sometimes they go *tramp, tramp, tramp,* keeping time with their feet before the music starts. Well, that's music, too.

"Then maybe you come around to that old creaking-door sound again. You know people like what's familiar to them, and that old creaking-door sound has already been introduced to them. It's an old friend, so you can bring it in again and folks are glad to hear it."

"Then you edge into the sound that old door made when it shut. You don't jump into it suddenly. It's not a good idea to jump right into things, ever. You got to smooth the way a little. Suppose you want to ask Aunt Selina for a taste of that chocolate cake she's just made. You don't just bounce right in and say, 'Gimme some cake!' If you do, you're not likely to get any. No, sir! You say, 'Good morning, Aunt Selina!' real polite. After that, you tell her what a wonderful cook she is, and then you just remark that there's nothing in the world any better than her chocolate cake. You see, that puts her in a good humor, and you go on from there toward getting your piece of cake."

"I see," said Chris, greatly impressed.

"So you just glide into that old door sound with a few easy notes, like this—"

"And you slide down with an echo of the same sound—"

"Now, how does it sound so far?" Uncle Benny played the verse from the beginning.

"It sounds fine!" exclaimed Chris and Lucy.

"Well, then, all we need for your verse is a good ending," said Uncle Benny. "Let's all listen and see if we can get an idea. A good ending is mighty important."

Everybody cocked their ears. They heard roosters crowing at the big house, the wind whirring through the myrtle trees, some insects buzzing in the bushes. Near by two catbirds were scolding at each other with harsh voices, but nothing held any promise of a good ending.

Then down the road, coming nearer and nearer, they heard the slow plod of a horse's hoofs, and the heavy lumbering of a wooden cart. A Negro boy was driving, sitting on top of a load of snowy cotton. As the cart came past the house the boy took a harmonica out of his pocket and began to blow some mournful notes. There was no beginning and no ending, just the same sounds over and over again—

"How about that for an ending?" Chris asked hopefully.

"It sounds pretty mournful to me," said Lucy. "For the verse we want something lively I should say."

"Well, why not pep it up?" demanded Chris.

"But it has no ending," objected Lucy. "It just hangs in the air."

"It's not much trouble to put an ending to it," said Uncle Benny. "Liven it up a little, like Chris says, add a note to end it, and let's see how it'll sound—"

"It sounds all right!" Chris nodded approvingly.

"Now I'll play it all from beginning to end." Uncle Benny hummed the tune as he strummed.

"Just right!" said Lucy.

"Well, then, now that's finished, we'll see what we can do for your chorus. For that, it seems to me you want a lonesome tune," he added. "Lonesome?" echoed Lucy.

"You're talking about something lonesome in your song, aren't you? Something far away and lonely?"

"Why, yes, we are," Lucy admitted.

"Well, then, we've got to think up some lonesome tunes."

"What's a lonesome tune?" inquired Chris.

"Here's a lonesome tune. I don't remember the words to this one but I can hum it for you." Uncle Benny plucked some chords and began to hum.

"Yes, it does have a lonesome sound," said Lucy.

"And, listen! It almost fits our verses!" Chris sang a few lines of their song.

"So it does!" Uncle Benny agreed. "I tell you what, we might just use this song for a framework to build on. That basket there's got a framework of hickory splints. The bulrushes are woven around it. A house has got a framework of beams and uprights and so on, and the boards are nailed onto it. A tune is just like everything else, I reckon. It needs a framework, too. So we build on this tune, same swing, same length and so on. We could just start out with those first two notes, like this—"

"Then instead of going up, like that song does, let's drop down like people's feelings always do when they're lonesome and sad—"

When the old man paused and looked puzzled, Chris inquired, "What next?"

"I don't know what next. Step outside and see if you hear sounds that might give us an idea."

Both children stepped out onto the porch of the little cabin and stood listening.

"Do you hear anything out there?" called Uncle Benny.

"There's a mourning dove cooing back in the woods," replied Lucy. "He makes a sad call. He sort of moans in what my music teacher calls a minor key—"

"Maybe that's just the sound you need in your song." Uncle Benny brought his guitar outside and sat down on the porch. "Let's go *tramp, tramp, tramping* along on one note, then bring in that dove call, like this—"

"You know you haven't got to have fancy notes all the time. Tunes are something like layer cakes. It's the plain part that makes you appreciate the filling. Well, then, we slide on up and play it again, this time a little different—"

"Then we take the first part again and make an ending—"

"That's all. Easy as falling off a log! Now here it goes all the way through—"

"Oh, that's fine!" cried Lucy. "It's just what we wanted!"

"And it fits our tune exactly!" Chris added happily.

"Now I'll play it through whilst you sing your song."

Uncle Benny plucked a few chords and the children began. It went perfectly.

"That's a pretty good song," Uncle Benny nodded enthusiastically. "It sure is. Who's going to play for you on the Showboat?"

"You play for us, Uncle Benny," Lucy said. "It sounds fine with your guitar."

"Why, sure," said Uncle Benny, grinning with pleasure. "On the night the Showboat comes, I'll be all dressed up and ready to play for you."

During the rest of the week Chris and Lucy practiced their song. Uncle Benny practiced with them, plunking merrily away while they sang.

"When you walk out on the stage to sing your song," he told them, "you ought to make a little bow—so!" Then he showed them how to do it. "And the same when you get through singing. Now let's see you do it."

Lucy and Chris did it over and over again.

"Now don't sing your song for anybody and don't talk about it," warned Uncle Benny. "Talk about it and talk is all it'll amount to."

"No, no, we won't sing it for anybody and we won't talk about it," promised Chris and Lucy.

Saturday came at last. The Showboat would arrive that afternoon and the song contest would be held that night. Chris and Lucy were too excited to have a nap after lunch as they usually did.

"Oh, Mama, do let us go early to see the Showboat come

in," Chris begged. "It's a wonderful sight to see it come in!"

"But you'd miss your supper if you did that. You'd have to go at three or four o'clock and the show doesn't begin until seven."

"We'll buy some crackers and cheese at the store," said Chris.

"And we'll get dressed before we go," Lucy added.

"I suppose it's all right," Mama said. "We'll bring Uncle Benny in the carriage with us later. But do keep your clothes clean if you're going to sing tonight."

"We will," promised Chris and Lucy.

They dashed up to their rooms and dressed themselves in their best clothes. Then they ran to the little ditch behind the barn, where *Skeeter* was tied up. They loosed the boat and climbed hurriedly in.

What a swash of white foam streamed out behind as they rowed down the canal! The tall leaves of the irises and cat-tails waved furiously as they swept past. They swung around the curves of the creek, shot past the old ruined saw-mill, the cotton gin and the back yards of Bayview, and came at last to the wharf in front of Midgett's Store.

Their skiff scraped the sides of Mr. Silverthorne's oyster schooner as they came into the dock. Immediately a head popped out of the little cabin.

"Hi, there, children!" Mr. Silverthorne greeted them. "Come down to see the Showboat come in?"

"Sure have," cried Chris and Lucy.

Mr. Silverthorne climbed out, stood on top of his cabin and peered down the river.

"There she comes, all right!" he exclaimed. "There she comes!"

Chris and Lucy hastily tied *Skeeter* to the piling and climbed up beside Mr. Silverthorne.

Far down the river the Showboat was moving.

"Yes! There she comes! There she comes!" they shouted, jumping up and down with excitement.

Far down the river, like a brightly colored flower floating on the blue water, the Showboat was moving slowly along. Its gay awnings and flags fluttered in the breeze, its white paint gleamed in the sun.

"Yea! There she comes! There she comes!"

HERE COMES THE SHOWBOAT!

Mr. Midgett came running out of the store, his fat little stomach jouncing up and down with every step. People loafing on the store porch left their checker games and rushed out on the wharf. Everybody in Bayview came hurrying to see the Showboat come in.

On moved the great flatboat, slowly and smoothly, pulled along by a busy, puffing little tugboat. Soon it was close enough to see the show people standing on the top deck. They waved in a friendly manner to the crowd gathered on the dock. In ordinary clothes they were not very different from other people, Chris and Lucy thought. It was queer how different they looked on the stage—as bright and as glittering as butterflies.

"Hi ya!" A boy waved at Chris.

"Hi ya, pal!" the man beside him called out.

Chris stared in surprise. It was the man and the boy who had teased him about the bullfrogs.

"Hi!" Chris grinned and waved back.

The people on the bank seemed greatly impressed that he should know someone on the Showboat.

The little tug puffed and pulled, and the great flatboat was slowly maneuvered into the dock, on the other side from Mr. Silverthorne's oyster boat. Then all the Showboat people disappeared from the upper deck. Through the windows of a lower deck, they could be seen filing into a small room and sitting down at a long table.

"They're having supper!" said Mr. Midgett in surprise.

Chris and Lucy looked. The Showboat people were drinking coffee, or maybe it was yaupon tea, just like anybody else! What a wonderful thing it must be to live on a Showboat and have breakfast in one town and dinner in another and supper in another! And to dress up every night in those beautiful clothes and act on the stage!

Chris and Lucy began to sing.

The light in the sky began to fade away. People went back to their homes. Chris and Lucy bought some crackers and cheese and a bottle of pickles from Mr. Midgett's store, and sat down upon the bank in the twilight and had their picnic supper.

Then it grew dark. Somewhere on the Showboat a motor

started and electric lights flashed on. Soon the show would begin. The ticket booth was opening and the people began to cross the gangplank.

Mama and Papa arrived with Uncle Benny. Mama combed Lucy's hair and tied it with a pink ribbon. She tied a pink sash about her dress. Chris combed his hair. They noticed that Uncle Benny was wearing a fine new necktie that Papa had given him for the occasion. Then, full of excitement, they bought their tickets and trooped into the theater. They sat near the front so that Chris and Lucy and Uncle Benny would be near the stage when their turn came. They sat on the edges of their seats, titillating with excitement.

At last the curtain went up and the show began.

Some very lovely ladies, all dressed in fluffy ruffles, sang a lively song and kicked their heels higher than Chris or Lucy had ever thought it possible to kick. Then, to their surprise, the man and the boy who had spoken to them from the deck of the Showboat, came on the stage. The man picked a twangy piece on a banjo and the boy did a fancy clog dance that made his feet move too fast to be seen. It was astonishing. Next came a little play that was very funny. Everyone howled with laughter. Then at last the curtain went down.

When it went up again, the scenery had been changed. There was a backdrop with a little rose-covered cottage painted on it. At one side a great poster was propped on an easel. OLD HOME SINGING CONTEST it said in glittering letters.

A master of ceremonies came upon the stage and asked everyone who wished to take part in the contest to come through the little side door which would take them backstage.

THE SHOWBOAT

"Oh, gee!" exclaimed Chris. "We'll see what it's like back there!" It was something he had always wondered about.

A number of people got up and went timidly toward the door, Chris and Lucy and Uncle Benny among them. It was dim and cluttered behind the scenes, with canvas scenery stacked against the walls. They could look out through the wings and see the master of ceremonies still talking. Then at last the contest began.

The first who performed was Miss Minnie, the dressmaker. She went out, draped in a sheet, and sang *Rock of Ages* with many beautiful gestures. People clapped and applauded. It was very pretty. Then Mrs. Midgett, the storekeeper's wife, played the zither and sang a long, doleful song about a beautiful lady who was drowned in a millpond. People all through the audience began to sniffle. It was very sad.

Mr. Saw-fiddle Saddler went next and fiddled away while he sang:

> "Oh, I wish I was single again,
>   For when I was single my pockets did jingle,
>   Oh, I wish I was single again!"

People whistled and clapped and laughed.

Chris and Lucy, who stood at the very end of the line, began to feel discouraged. Everyone who performed seemed to them better than the last. They could not possibly win that prize, they thought. They wondered dismally if anybody would clap for them.

At last the master of ceremonies beckoned to them. They got up, walked out upon the stage and made their little bow as Uncle Benny had taught them.

HERE COMES THE SHOWBOAT!

The glare of the footlights was so bright that they could not see anybody in the audience. Uncle Benny took a chair that was offered him and struck up the lively music. Immediately, Chris and Lucy felt better. Their song was good after all!

They began to sing.

I

We went to the conjure man one day
And took some collards for his pay,
He gave to me an old horseshoe,
A smelly charm to Sister Lu.

Chorus

Way down yonder where the rivers flow,
Way down yonder where the rushes blow,
Way down yonder in Pasquotank,
Where the bullfrogs jump from bank to bank,
Way down yonder in Pasquotank!

2

We thought for sure they'd bring us luck,
But listen, folks, how we were stuck:
Our calf got mad and with a pitch
Dumped us both into the ditch.

Chorus

3

And when Chris went to go to bed
That horseshoe conked him on the head,
But Sister Lu said, "Let's not fret,
I've got my bag of good luck yet."

Chorus

4

She went to church and people said,
"Surely, there is something dead!"
The preacher sniffed the awful smell
And said it was the fumes of hell!

                                        Chorus

5

Then tattletaling Mittie Belle
Got up and said, "No, it ain't hell.
And there's nobody dead today,
It's Lucy's asafetida!"

                                        Chorus

6

And so we say in great disgust
The conjure man's an awful bust.
We'll make our luck as best we can
And never trust a conjure man!

                                        Chorus

How the people clapped and shouted as Chris and Lucy finished their song! How they laughed! For the tale of the trip to the conjure man had got around.

"You've made a hit!" the master of ceremonies cried, clapping and clapping with the others.

Chris and Lucy bowed again and again as the applause went on and on. Then they marched happily from the stage.

"Oh, do you think we've won?" whispered Lucy to Chris excitedly.

"You never can tell!" he whispered back.

They waited anxiously while the master of ceremonies

and several members of the Showboat troupe withdrew to judge the songs. In a very short while they returned. The master of ceremonies stepped to the front of the stage.

"We've decided to award the prize," he announced importantly, "to the song that was made up especially for the occasion, *Way Down Yonder in Pasquotank*. Will Christopher and Lucy Gale please step forward?"

In a haze of joy, Chris and Lucy walked out on the stage again.

"Since there are two of you," the master of ceremonies said, smiling at them, "the Showboat is going to give you two prizes, one for you," he placed a five-dollar gold piece in Lucy's hand, "and one for you," he placed another in Chris's.

"Oh, thank you!" cried Chris and Lucy together. They could hardly believe their good luck.

"We'll buy something fine for Uncle Benny!" Lucy whispered joyfully to Chris.

The children looked down at the shining gold pieces. That wonderful set of doll's furniture and those fancy cowboy boots were in the bag!

"*Way down yonder where the rivers flow,*" sang the audience gleefully, as Chris and Lucy marched from the stage.

And the rafters rang with the music:

"Way down yonder where the rushes blow,
Way down yonder in Pasquotank,
Where the bullfrogs jump from bank to bank,
Way down yonder in Pasquotank!"

THE SHOWBOAT
WAY DOWN YONDER IN
PASQUOTANK

We went to the con-jure man one day. And took some col-lards for his pay. He gave to me an old horse-shoe, a smel-ly charm to Sis-ter—— Lu. Way down yon—der where the riv-ers flow.—— Way down yon-der where the rush-es blow.—— Way down yon-der in Pas — quo — tank Where the bullfrogs jump from bank—— to bank, Way down yon-der in Pas-quo — tank.——